Power Forward

WRITTEN BY TRACEY WEST

DISNEY PRESS

New York

Content of book was developed in consultation with Lilly USA, LLC
and is funded by Lilly USA, LLC.

First Edition

10 9 8 7 6 5 4 3 2 1

ISBN 978-1-4231-4705-3
J689-1817-1-11244
PRINTED IN USA
LILLY IS A REGISTERED TRADEMARK OF ELI LILLY AND COMPANY.
ALL RIGHTS RESERVED.

**Looking for tips on family life with type 1 diabetes?
Visit www.family.com/type1**

For more Disney Press fun, visit www.disneybooks.com

Power Forward

Chapter 1

Justin Cooper tore down the basketball court, trying to keep up with Marcus Flint, the point guard. Marcus was shorter than Justin, but the kid could really move. Justin tried to get past him, but Marcus was just too fast.

Just past the foul line, Marcus stopped and took a shot at the basket. The ball hit the edge of the rim and bounced back. Justin was on it. He jumped up, caught the rebound, and quickly took the shot.

Swish! The ball sailed through the hoop. The shrill sound of a whistle bounced off the concrete walls of the gym.

"That's game! Great scrimmage, guys," Coach Perez called out.

"I've been watching what you guys can do," he said. "I've got to say, this is one of the best seventh-grade teams I've seen in a long time. It hasn't been easy to choose a team captain. There are a lot of talented and dedicated players on this team. But one of you has stood out more than anyone else. And that player is . . . Justin Cooper!"

Justin opened his eyes. Team captain! That had been the most amazing moment of his life. But had it really only been last week? It seemed like ages ago. Justin felt as if his whole life had fallen apart since then. He had just been diagnosed with type 1 diabetes.

Justin looked around. He was sitting in

a sterile, white doctor's office. His parents were talking quietly in the corner. They had been told that a diabetes nurse would be with them soon, but it felt as if it were taking *years* for her to show up.

Justin's cell phone buzzed in his pocket. He took it out to see a text message from Mike Vantine.

Dude, where r u?

Mike was Justin's best friend and basketball teammate. Or was it former teammate? Could Justin even play basketball anymore? What if he had to give it up? He had worked so hard; what if his diabetes ruined everything?

Justin stared at the phone. He had no idea what to say to Mike. Sighing, he put the phone back in his pocket without responding.

Finally the door opened and a friendly-looking woman with short black hair came in.

"You must be Justin," she said. "I'm Kendra Diaz, your diabetes nurse educator."

"Hi, Kendra," Mr. Cooper said, holding out his hand. "I'm Harry Cooper, and this is my wife, Denise."

"It's good to meet you," Kendra said warmly, shaking Mr. Cooper's hand.

Justin looked at his dad. His shirt was wrinkled from being in the doctor's office for what seemed like forever, and he looked tired. His dad's clothing was never wrinkled. He even ironed his socks! But his dad didn't even seem to notice the wrinkles. Seeing him look so unlike himself, Justin felt uneasy all over again.

"I know this is scary and confusing for you right now, but that's why I'm here," Kendra said, breaking into Justin's thoughts. "Dr. Chang told me she talked to you a bit about your diagnosis, but there's definitely more to learn. But first, do you have any questions?"

Justin's parents looked at him, encouraging him to speak up. He didn't feel much like talking, but Kendra was right. He *did* have a lot of questions.

"Dr. Chang said a lot of stuff, but I didn't really get it," Justin answered. "Like, what does having diabetes *mean*?"

"Our bodies need energy every day, to think, to play, to work," Kendra said. "Every time we eat, our body breaks that food down into glucose, or sugar. That's what the body uses for energy. In order for the glucose to get into your cells, where it can be used, your body has to make a hormone called insulin. Insulin allows the cells to use the glucose and keeps your blood sugar from getting too high.

"Type 1 diabetes is a disease that causes your body to stop making insulin. When that happens, your blood sugar gets out of control. That's what's been going on with you. And that's where we come in. We can help you learn how to balance your insulin, food, and physical activity to help control your blood sugar."

"So he'll have to take insulin shots?" Mrs. Cooper asked.

Kendra nodded. "Yes. But I'm going to help all of you learn how to do that."

Justin was freaking out. When you got sick, you were supposed to get better, right? Like when he got a cold. He felt really bad for a couple of days, and then when it was over he didn't even remember how bad it was.

Kendra noticed the worried look on his face. "Lots of kids just like you live with diabetes every day, Justin. You can still do the things you love to do, like play basketball."

"How did you know I play basketball?" Justin asked.

6

"Dr. Chang told me," Kendra answered. "And that's great. Getting exercise is important for everybody, especially when you have diabetes. I'm sure you'll be back on the court soon."

Hearing that made Justin feel a little better—but just a little.

"Before you go home today, we're going to teach you some important information, including how to give yourself an insulin shot," Kendra continued. "But first I'm going to send my friend Lisa in to talk with you. She's a dietitian, and she'll help you figure out the best things for you to eat."

Kendra turned to Mr. and Mrs. Cooper. "We'll give you lots of support," she promised. "By the time you leave today, you and Justin should be comfortable with handling the basics of his diabetes. And we'll meet with you at the diabetes center several times over the next few days for follow-up classes."

"Let me get this straight," Justin said. "Not only do I have to get shots every day, I get extra school, too?"

"The classes won't last forever," Kendra told him. "And besides, I think you'll find they help you a lot."

Kendra looked down at the clipboard she carried. "Let me go get Lisa, and I'll see you in a little while."

Kendra left the room, and Justin's mom gave him a weak smile.

"Well, she's nice, isn't she?" Mrs. Cooper asked.

Justin turned his head and stared at the wall. "There's nothing nice about this," he muttered.

Chapter 2

Justin heard a knock, and then the door to the room opened.

"Hi, Justin. I'm Lisa, the dietitian Kendra told you about. How are you feeling?"

Justin turned to see a woman who reminded him of his grandma. She was short, with curly gray hair.

"Pretty confused," Justin answered truthfully. "And nervous. Am I going to have to go on a special diet? Will I have to give up all my favorite foods?"

"Well, that's what I'm here to talk to you about. Managing your diabetes is all about keeping a balance between your insulin, the food you eat, and your physical activity. Having diabetes doesn't mean you have to buy special diet foods. It's about making healthy food choices. How you eat now will determine the changes you may need to make. We'll talk about your favorite foods in one of our classes and make sure you can still include them. You will need to become more aware of what's in the food you eat, how much you eat, and the time you eat in relation to when you take your insulin, but that's what I'm here to help with."

Over the next half hour, Lisa asked Justin a lot of questions about what he ate and how much, when he usually ate, and his physical activity throughout the day. She explained that knowing what he was eating would help her in making suggestions about changes he could make to better manage his diabetes. She also explained that he would need to be consistent with his eating and follow a pretty tight schedule until they could determine how his body reacted to food, activity, and insulin. Once they understood that, they would be able to start making adjustments for everyday things like trying new food or going out to eat with friends. The consistent meals would also give Justin and his parents time to learn how to plan his own meals, measure his food and estimate portion sizes, count carbs, and so on. Justin tried to keep up with it all, but it was a lot to take in. He was glad his parents were there.

Lisa saw the confused look on Justin's face. "I know it's a lot of information," she said. "I don't expect you to remember it all right now. We'll go over it again in your diabetes classes. I promise it will all start to make sense soon."

Lisa gave Justin some pamphlets to read and said she would see him tomorrow.

A few minutes later, Kendra came back in. "I'm going to take you through some important information," she told Justin.

Kendra held up a small, shaped box with a digital screen. "This is a blood glucose meter. It measures the amount of glucose in your blood, or your blood sugar. Keeping track of your blood sugar is an important part of managing your diabetes, so you'll need to know how and when to use the meter."

Kendra handed the blood glucose meter to Justin, and talked him through how to use it. Justin felt kind of weird about pricking his finger with the lancet, but he did it anyway. He followed the rest of Kendra's instructions and a number came up on the screen.

Kendra showed Justin the screen and

explained what the number meant. Then she looked at Mr. and Mrs. Cooper. "The next step is teaching you how to give Justin his shot. He'll be able to do it on his own soon, but for now we need to know that one of you can give him his injections."

Kendra and Justin's parents practiced until Mr. and Mrs. Cooper felt comfortable that they could give Justin a shot at home.

"Justin will need to take a shot before his meals, and one before bedtime," Kendra told Mr. and Mrs. Cooper. "I know this is a lot to take in, but I'll give you the number for the diabetes center. Until you learn how to adjust his insulin on your own, you should call in his blood sugar and they'll tell you over the phone how much insulin to give Justin. You'll review all of this in your first class tomorrow, too. Soon you'll all be pros at adjusting Justin's insulin."

Kendra turned to Justin. "I'm sure you're

nervous about giving yourself your own shots. We'll go over it with you in class and make sure you feel comfortable before you do it yourself. For now, your parents or a nurse will be able to help you out."

Mrs. Cooper sighed. "This is all so confusing."

Kendra nodded. "I know. But you're not alone in this. You have a whole team ready to help if you need it."

"Can I go home now?" Justin asked.

"We're almost there," Kendra replied. "Before you leave, I need to make sure you and your parents know the signs and symptoms of high and low blood sugar and what to do if that happens."

As Kendra went through a booklet that explained the symptoms, Justin felt like he was back in science class. He was relieved when Kendra finally said they could go home.

"I'll see you tomorrow morning, Justin," Kendra told him.

"Will I be here all day?" Justin asked. "Because I have practice tomorrow."

"Sorry, Justin, but practice will have to wait for about a week," Kendra said. "You'll have to miss some school, too."

Justin started to panic. "But I can't miss practice. I'm captain!"

"Coach Perez will understand," his mom assured him.

Justin felt his cheeks get hot. He was really upset. "But the guys won't."

"Honey, you've got diabetes," she said. "They'll understand."

"I promise that Dr. Chang and I will get you back on the court, Justin," Kendra assured him. "But we need to make sure you'll be safe. Okay?"

"Yeah," Justin muttered. But it didn't feel okay.

The captain couldn't miss practice for a week. That wasn't cool. And it was all because of stupid diabetes.

It was ruining his whole life!

Chapter 3

The next morning Justin's mom woke him up early. Justin groaned and pulled his pillow over his head.

"I thought I didn't have to go to school," he complained.

"It's already eight thirty," Mrs. Cooper said. "We've got to go to the diabetes center this morning."

Justin reluctantly climbed out of bed and got dressed. When he got downstairs, the delicious smell of eggs and bacon reached his nose. Justin reached out to grab a piece of bacon from the stove.

"Not so fast," his dad said. "You've got to check your blood sugar before you eat, remember?"

"How am I supposed to remember?" Justin asked. "I just got diabetes yesterday."

"That's funny. You can remember every basketball play your coach teaches you," Mr. Cooper kidded him.

Justin sighed and got the glucose monitor from the kitchen counter. He checked his blood sugar and showed the numbers to his mom, who gave him his insulin shot and noted the information in his logbook.

After breakfast they went to the diabetes center, where Justin's diabetes team worked. There were lots of different diabetes doctors and nurses there.

Justin and his parents started their day

with Lisa, the dietitian. Now that Justin was feeling a little less overwhelmed, he found it easier to concentrate on what she was saying. Lisa explained to Justin the importance of balancing his meals with his physical activity and insulin. She explained how different foods affected his blood sugar, how to estimate portion sizes for what he was eating, and how to figure out the amount of carbohydrate in his foods. Mr. Cooper took a lot of notes, and promised to call Lisa if they had any problems with Justin's meal plan.

Next Justin met with Kendra.

"It's good to see you, Justin," she said. "How did everything go this morning?"

"Okay, I guess," Justin said. "It's weird, though. I mean, I can't believe I have to check my blood sugar and take shots for the rest of my life."

Kendra nodded. "I know. It's a lot to take in. But the shots and checking your blood sugar are part of the whole plan to help you manage your diabetes. We need to help you learn how to properly balance your insulin with your exercise and the food you eat. That's why I want to talk about basketball today."

Justin felt nervous. "Wait—you said I could still play."

Kendra nodded. "And you can. Exercise is important for everyone to stay healthy, not just people with type 1 diabetes. But when you have diabetes, you have to understand how things affect your blood sugar, too."

"Like what?" Justin asked.

"Physical activity like basketball can lower your blood sugar. Everyone's body reacts differently, so you'll want to keep an eye on it," Kendra explained. "We need to work up a plan for how often you should check your blood sugar during practice or a game. That will help you understand how your physical activity is affecting you, and what changes need to be made to your insulin or eating. I want to make sure you feel good about monitoring your blood sugar before you go back out there. If you exercise at home, be sure to note it in your logbook, and let us know how it went. We can use that information to develop a plan for practices and games."

Justin was relieved to hear that he could still play, even if he couldn't play with the team this week.

His final meeting of the day was with a social worker named Pam.

Pam was an older woman in jeans and a sweater with animals on it. Justin thought she looked like a kindergarten teacher. He wasn't exactly sure why she was there. Was she going to make him finger-paint or something?

Pam gave him a big smile. "Hi, Justin. You've been through a lot, huh?"

"That's for sure," Justin replied.

"You're probably feeling a lot of different things right now," she said. "But you should know that you're not alone. Lots of kids have type 1 diabetes."

Oh, no, Justin thought. *She wants to talk about feelings*. He always hated it when his mom tried to get him to talk about his feelings. It was much easier to keep them inside. He didn't feel like talking. He'd spent all morning at the diabetes center. Now he just wanted to go home!

Pam told Justin a lot about talking to other kids with diabetes online, or even meeting with them in a group. He just kept responding with, "Sure. Yeah. Right," but he didn't mean it. The last thing he wanted to do right now was talk to other kids. The fewer people who knew about this, the better.

After what felt like ages, Pam finally left the room and Justin was able to go home.

In the car, Justin's mom turned to talk to him in the backseat. "After we get home, I'm going to the school to talk to Principal Natelli and the school nurse," she said. "Kendra gave me some pamphlets I can give them in case they haven't dealt with diabetes before. I'll fill in Coach Perez, too, but I'll leave it up to you to tell your friends and your teammates."

"What do you mean?" Justin asked. "Why do I have to tell them? It's none of their business."

Mr. Cooper looked at him in the rearview mirror. "You know, last night I was reading some blogs written by kids with type 1 diabetes. A lot of them said it helped to talk to other kids with diabetes, because they share the same feelings."

Feelings. There was that stupid word again. Justin shook his head. "No way. I do *not* want the team to know. Tell Coach Perez not to tell them, okay?"

His mom sighed. "It's up to you, Justin. But I hope you'll think about it some more. Why don't you want them to know?"

Justin shrugged. "I just don't."

But his thoughts were more complicated than that. He was team captain. Captains needed to be strong, not weak. What if his team thought his diabetes made him weak? What if they decided they wanted a new captain—one who wasn't sick?

He was going to keep his diabetes a secret, no matter what.

Chapter 4

Justin decided that even if he couldn't practice all week, he could still help the team. When he got home, he changed into his uniform and shot some hoops in the driveway for a half hour. Then he went into the kitchen and grabbed a sports drink from the refrigerator.

Before he could drink it, his mom walked into the kitchen and took it out of his hands. "Hold on there. You need to know how many carbs are in there before you drink it."

"Seriously?" Justin asked. "I always drink this when I practice."

"You can still have it if you want this to be your snack. But you need to think about how it might affect your blood sugar. This bottle has more carbs than Lisa's plan calls for in a snack," she said, showing Justin the label. "Why not pick something else for right now?"

Justin couldn't believe it. "You mean I can never drink it again?"

"Of course you can. But remember what Lisa said? Right now it's important to stick as close as possible to your meal plan so we can figure out how your body reacts to food, insulin, and physical activity. We'll learn how to work these things in. It will just take some time. Next time we see Lisa, we'll be sure to ask about how to incorporate this into your meal plan. But for now, I think it's best to avoid sports drinks."

"That is so lame!" Justin moaned. "I can't believe I have to watch everything that goes in my mouth!" Justin grabbed one of his snacks off the counter and stomped out of the kitchen. He flopped on the living room couch and turned the TV on, raising the volume to drown out everything around him.

Mrs. Cooper followed him into the living room and lowered the sound. "You know, this would be a good time to go on those blogs your dad checked out," she suggested.

"I don't know," Justin said. "It sounds kind of boring."

Besides, what does it matter how many other kids have diabetes? he thought to himself. *It's not going to change anything. I still have diabetes.*

His mom shrugged. "I hope you change

your mind. But if you're not going to check out the blogs, you can help me with our weekly meal plan."

"No offense, but that sounds even more boring than those blogs," Justin said.

"Tough," his mom said. "Besides, if you help me then maybe we can make sure it isn't so 'lame.'"

Justin rolled his eyes. "Yeah, right!" he said, but he headed to the table to help. He wanted to make sure his mom didn't fill his meals with stuff he hated to eat.

It took the rest of the afternoon to make the meal plan. Justin would never admit it, but he actually found it kind of interesting. It was almost like making a game plan. And it turned out that he really liked most of the foods they decided on.

Around five o'clock, the doorbell rang. Justin answered it. It was Mike.

His friend held out an envelope. "I got

your homework," he said. "Dude, what's wrong with you?"

Justin thought quickly. "It's like a flu or something," he lied. "I have to stay in the house so I don't infect anybody."

Mike took a big step backward. "Then quit breathing on me! I don't need your germs, man," he joked.

Justin laughed. "Hey, how was practice today?"

"Good," Mike said. "Everyone was wondering where you were. Coach let Marcus call the drills."

Justin felt a pang in his gut. "No way. Did he make Marcus captain instead of me?"

Mike shook his head. "No. He said it was just until you get back. You coming tomorrow?"

Justin shook his head. "They want me out for, like, a week."

Mike frowned. "You don't look sick."

"Yeah, it's one of those flus that sneaks up

on you," Justin lied again. "You don't even know you have it."

"All right," Mike said. "Guess I'll see you tomorrow."

"Okay," Justin said.

He watched Mike run off before he closed the door. He didn't like lying to him. Mike was his best friend, but he couldn't keep a secret. Just last month, Mike's dad had tried to throw a big surprise birthday party for his mom. Mike couldn't stand the suspense and had told his mom all about it. If Mike knew about his diabetes, the whole team would know.

His dad walked up behind him. "Homework?" he asked, looking down at the envelope. Justin nodded. "Well, at least you won't be bored," Mr. Cooper said.

"Ha. Very funny," Justin replied. What good was staying out of school if you still had to do homework?

But Justin did his homework. And he read the brochures Kendra had sent home with him, especially the ones that talked about having diabetes and playing sports. On Tuesday, Kendra asked if he was ready to try giving himself his own shot.

"I guess so," Justin replied. With Kendra and his parents watching over him, Justin checked his blood sugar. Then Kendra helped his mom prepare his insulin, and Justin injected himself with it. It hurt, but Justin was actually pretty proud of himself for doing it on his own.

"I knew you were gonna ace this," Kendra said with a smile. "It gets easier the more you practice—kind of like basketball."

"I'd still rather be playing basketball," Justin said.

Kendra laughed. "That's for sure. Hey, have a good night. I'll see you tomorrow."

On Wednesday, Justin and his mom met

with Kendra again. She had her clipboard out, and she asked Justin a lot of questions. What time did he wake up? Did he play any other sports besides basketball? How many times a week did he practice? Stuff like that.

"It's important for us to know what your life is like," Kendra explained. "The more we know, the better we'll be able to help you manage your diabetes."

"Can you really do that?" Justin asked.

Kendra nodded. "And we're going to start by making a schedule you can follow once you go back to school and practice."

Justin shook his head as they filled out the boxes on the schedule.

"This looks like an evil math test," he joked.

Kendra laughed. "That's why we're writing it down. This way you won't forget!"

When they got home, Justin went to his driveway basketball court to do some drills

before lunch. He did laps around the driveway to warm up. Then he practiced running
up to the basket and shooting—over and
over again.

All of a sudden, he felt light-headed. His
stomach felt queasy. Something wasn't right.
His heart started to pound fast as he stumbled into the house.

"Mom, I feel weird," Justin called out.

His mom ran up to him. "You look pale.
Let's check your blood sugar."

Justin sat down on the couch while
his mother ran for the glucose meter. She
quickly pricked his finger.

"Your blood sugar's low," she said. "Kendra
said that might happen when you're exercising, remember? Let me give you a few
glucose tablets and we'll recheck it."

Justin took the tablets. After fifteen minutes, he checked his blood sugar again.

"It's back in range," Justin said with relief.

"I'll give the diabetes center a call and let them know," his mom said. "But I think we handled it the right way."

The next day, Justin saw Dr. Chang again.

"Your mom told me what happened when you were playing basketball yesterday," she said. "It can be scary at first. But now you know some symptoms to look out for. Next time, when you start to feel light-headed, you need to stop what you're doing and check your blood sugar."

"I will," Justin promised.

Dr. Chang looked down at her chart. "Otherwise, Justin, it seems like you're getting good at checking your blood sugar," she told him.

"I'm injecting my own insulin and everything now," Justin bragged.

"That's awesome," Dr. Chang said. "So, when's your next practice?"

"Well, there's one today after school," Justin replied. "And Saturday morning."

Dr. Chang looked at him. "Tell you what," she said. "I think you're ready to go to school tomorrow. And if that goes okay, you can go to practice on Saturday. Let's just review a few things first, okay?"

Justin nodded. "Let's do this. I know it." He'd actually been paying attention all week, not like the first day at the doctor's office.

Dr. Chang turned to Justin. "So, what should you do before practice?"

"Put on my uniform," Justin replied. Dr. Chang raised an eyebrow, and he grinned. "Just kidding. Check my blood sugar."

"Good," she said. "Anything else?"

"Eat a snack if I need it to cover the extra activity," Justin replied.

"Good. Here's an important one," Dr. Chang said. "What should you do if you feel light-headed or have other symptoms of a low during the game?"

"Stop playing and check my blood sugar," he replied.

Dr. Chang smiled. "Are you sure you want to be a basketball pro when you grow up? You'd make a great diabetes doctor."

"So does that mean I can go to practice Saturday?" Justin asked.

She nodded. "As long as everything goes well at school tomorrow, I don't see why not."

Justin felt like running around the room, he was so happy. Dr. Chang looked at his dad.

"You should make sure his coach knows all this," she reminded Mr. Cooper.

Mr. Cooper nodded. "We made a checklist for him and we have a meeting to go over everything in person tomorrow. He's been really great."

"Then you're good to go, Justin," Dr. Chang said. "I'll see you next week."

Justin couldn't wait to get back to practice. He didn't even mind going back to school. He just wanted things to be normal again.

On Friday morning, Justin realized that "normal" was going to be different from now on. During the week, he had gotten used to the changes in his schedule. But now things had to change again to match his school schedule. His mom woke him up fifteen minutes earlier than she used to on a school day to make sure he had enough time to check his blood sugar and give himself his shot. When Justin was finally ready to leave, he picked up his backpack. It felt like it was filled with bricks.

"Mom, this is, like, a hundred pounds," Justin said. "What's in here?"

37

"You've got to be prepared all the time," Mrs. Cooper reminded him. "I've packed some things in case your blood sugar gets low, plus your snack to have before practice, and some extras just in case you need them."

Justin unzipped his backpack. Besides his lunch bag, there were three apples, a bag of trail mix, and two juice boxes.

Justin shook his head. "There's a whole grocery store in here!" he said.

"Well, maybe I went a little overboard," his mom admitted. "But I'm new at this. Anyway, don't forget. Your meter is in your second pocket along with the schedule we made with Kendra. Nurse Myers will help you give yourself your shot before lunch. Okay?"

"I got it, Mom," Justin said impatiently. "I'm gonna miss the bus."

Justin got outside just as the bus pulled up in front of his house. Mike was in their usual seat in the next-to-last row. Justin sat down next to him.

"I'm glad you're back," Mike said. "I was getting tired of bringing your homework to you every night."

Marcus was sitting in the backseat with his two best friends, Jeremy Kim and Terrell Crawford. He leaned over the seat and stuck his head between Justin and Mike.

"I heard you had swine flu," he said. "Gross, dude. What did you do, kiss a pig or something?"

Jeremy and Terrell laughed. They always laughed at anything Marcus said.

"My uncle had swine flu last year," Jeremy said. "He had to go to the hospital."

"I didn't have swine flu," Justin said, not looking at Marcus.

Marcus started to make a noise like a pig. "Oink! Oink! Oink!" Then he fell back in his seat, laughing.

"Whatever," Justin said.

Mike shook his head. "Jerks."

When they got to school, a few kids asked Justin where he had been all week, but nobody really made a big deal about it, which was cool. Then he got to first period English. Ms. McMahon looked at him with her eyes all big—the same look his mom gave him when she was feeling sappy.

"Justin, it's *so good* to have you back," she said dramatically. "Let me know if you need anything, okay?"

Justin held his breath. Was she going to talk about his diabetes? Because she definitely knew about it. Justin suddenly felt angry. Why did his teachers have to know, anyway?

After English, Justin headed to homeroom. He expected Mrs. Duffy to be all weird, too, but she acted perfectly normal. His math and art teachers were cool, too. Maybe he could keep his diabetes a secret after all.

Finally it was time for lunch. The other kids ran for the lunchroom, and Justin started to follow. He was halfway down the hall when he remembered.

"My shot," he muttered to himself. He went back to his locker and took out the small bag with the meter and stuff his mom had given him. Then he headed for Nurse Myers's office.

Justin had seen her once before when he had a stomachache. She seemed pretty nice. When he walked in, she was taking some kid's temperature. The boy was an eighth grader, and he didn't look so hot. His face was really pale.

Nurse Myers looked up. "Can I help you?" she asked. She was short, with curly brown hair and a round face. She was wearing a light blue nurse's coat over her regular clothes.

"Um, I'm um, I'm Justin Cooper," he said.

She nodded. "Hey, Justin. I'll be with you in a minute."

She took the thermometer from the boy and read it.

"One hundred and one," she said. "Why don't you go lie down in the back room? I'll tell the office to call your parents."

Justin waited while Nurse Myers made the call. Finally, she nodded to him.

"Your mom says you can check your own glucose and administer your own shot," she said. "I'll be supervising."

"Okay." Justin took out the meter and checked his blood sugar. He showed the number to the nurse, who began to prepare his insulin.

Justin nervously glanced at the open door.

"Um, could we close that?" he asked.

"Of course," Nurse Myers replied. "I'd take you into the other room, but poor Tommy's back there."

Justin quickly gave himself a shot in the leg. At the diabetes center, he had learned that it was good to rotate where he injected so he wasn't using the same place every time.

"All done," Nurse Myers said. "See you tomorrow, same time, same place."

"Thanks," Justin said. He left the office and raced back to his locker. He put his supplies away and grabbed his lunch bag.

But by the time he got to the cafeteria, most of the kids were already done eating. He saw Mike and some other guys heading out to the yard in the back. There was a basketball court out there. Every day after lunch they played a quick game of pickup.

"Dude, you coming?" Mike called out over the noisy lunch crowd.

Justin really, really, wanted to go. But he knew he had to eat. If he messed up today, his parents might not let him go to practice tomorrow.

Justin shook his head and found an empty table. He sat down and opened up his lunch bag. His mom had packed him ham and cheese, his favorite, but it didn't taste good. He was too angry.

Everyone kept saying that he could do all the stuff he liked with his diabetes. But instead of playing pickup, he was sitting by himself, eating a sandwich.

Chapter 5

"Are you sure you don't want me to stay?" Mrs. Cooper asked.

"Mom, I'm sure," Justin repeated. It was, like, the seventeenth time she'd asked him.

They were in the parking lot outside the school gym. Practice started in ten minutes, but the way his mom was acting, Justin wasn't sure she was going to let him go.

Mrs. Cooper took a deep breath. "All right. Coach Perez knows what to do if something happens. You've got everything in your bag, right?"

Justin held up a small black backpack. "Water bottle. Snacks. Blood sugar meter. Lancet. Strips. Glucose tablets. Check."

"Good," his mom said. "I'll pick you up at noon sharp. We've got a class at the diabetes center after lunch."

Justin saw his chance and quickly exited the car. "Thanks, Mom!" he called behind him as he ran to the gym. It felt good to run again.

A few of his teammates were already inside, shooting at the basket. Coach Perez stood on the sidelines, holding a clipboard. Tall, with dark crew-cut hair, Coach looked to Justin like he could play pro if he wanted. The coach nodded when he saw Justin.

"Hey, Cooper. Good to see you," he said.

Justin ran over to him. "Thanks, Coach."

"How's your blood sugar?" the coach asked in a low voice.

"It's good," Justin said. "I checked it before I came and it was fine. I had a snack, too."

Coach Perez nodded. "Good. I'm going to have you lead some drills today. Let me know if you're feeling bad or need a break, all right? And don't forget to check your blood sugar during practice."

"Wow, you sound like my mom," Justin said, and the coach grinned.

"You're not the first player I've coached who had diabetes," Coach Perez said. "I know the drill."

That surprised Justin. For the past week he'd been feeling like the only basketball player in the world with diabetes. He wanted to ask the coach more about the other players, but just then a bunch of his teammates ran into the gym. Justin didn't want them to overhear.

"Yo, Captain!" Logan Katz called out. "It's about time!"

Mike tossed him the ball, and Justin caught it. "Hope you didn't forget how a basketball works," his friend said.

"No way," Justin replied. He dribbled the ball past Mike and Logan, stopped at the foul line, spun around on his heel, and sunk a shot clean through the net.

Coach Perez blew his whistle. "All right, team, line up! Cooper's going to lead a couple of drills today. One passing, one shooting. His choice. Got that, Cooper?"

Justin nodded. This was the moment he'd been waiting for since the first time he'd held a basketball.

"Pass and go!" Justin called out, running onto the court. "One hundred times, no drops. Logan, you're in the middle first. Let's go!"

The pass and go drill was one of Justin's favorites. He liked the rhythm of it. The twelve boys on the team quickly formed a circle in the center of the court. Justin passed the ball to Logan and then ran to join him in the middle of the circle. Logan passed it to Mike and then ran to the empty space where Justin used to be. Mike passed the ball to Justin in the center, and the whole thing kept going until they made one hundred complete passes—or somebody missed.

Justin counted in his head as the boys went around the circle. He was up to forty-seven when Freddy Romano dropped the ball.

"Start over!" Justin called out, and some of the boys groaned. Justin didn't mind. As captain, you had to take stuff like that.

The second time went better, even though Marcus yelled, "Don't drop it this time!" every time someone threw the ball to Freddy.

"One hundred!" Justin called out after the final complete pass. "Nice job!"

Justin clapped his hands. "Okay, we need to pair up. Let's do some six-sets."

Marcus groaned. "Oh, man, we did those all week!"

Justin ignored him. He liked doing six-sets. You had to think on your feet.

Justin and Mike paired up and took a spot on the three-point line to the right of the basket. The other players paired up, too, and lined up behind them.

"All right, let's go!" Justin called out.

Mike took a shot from the three-point line. It bounced off the backboard into the basket. Justin retrieved the ball and passed it back to him. Mike moved in to catch the pass and tried a jump shot. This one hit the backboard, and Justin got the rebound. For his last shot, Mike went for a layup and made it. Justin passed the ball back to him again.

Mike and Justin moved up the three-point line, and Mike repeated all three shots. They kept moving around the line until Mike had shot from six different places.

After Mike's final shot, Justin passed the ball to Terrell. Then he and Mike ran to the back of the line. When it got back around to them, it would be Justin's turn to shoot and Mike's turn to rebound.

Justin always watched to see how the other guys were shooting, but now that he was captain, he paid extra attention. Marcus, as always, made every single shot. Darius Simmons only made a few, but man, it was hard to get past him when you were trying to get to the basket. They weren't all great shots, but everyone on the team was good at something.

Justin was so pumped to be back on the court that he only missed two shots during the whole drill. When he finished, Coach Perez blew his whistle.

"Let's do some defense now," the coach

called out. "Mike, Justin, Freddy, form a defensive line in front of the basket. Marcus is going to try to get past you. I want to see you stop him without making a foul."

Justin knew stopping Marcus wouldn't be easy. Coach Perez always said he could weave like a spider

"Just try to make a shot!" Freddy called out to Marcus.

Shot. Hearing the word out loud suddenly made Justin think of his diabetes. He was supposed to check his blood sugar during practice. What time was it, anyway? He looked to his left at the big clock above the bleachers. Ten to eleven. He still had time to . . .

"Wake up, Justin!" Marcus cried as he dribbled the ball right past him. He stopped under the net and sank an easy layup.

Justin clenched his fists. If he had been paying attention, he might have had a chance at stopping Marcus. Now he just looked like a fool.

"Let's see three more on the line!" Coach Perez called out.

Justin ran to the sidelines. He finished the rest of the drill, but his head just wasn't in it. He kept looking at the clock. 10:52 . . . 10:54 . . . He had to stick to the schedule that he and Kendra had worked out. He didn't want to mess up.

"Time for a scrimmage," Coach Perez announced. "Marcus, you're with Logan, Ryan, Jeremy, Terrell, and Noah. Justin, you've got Mike, Freddy, Darius, Luis, and Aaron."

Justin looked at the clock. "Be right back, Coach." He turned to Mike. "Take my position while I'm gone. Luis can play center."

Justin ran to the bleachers, grabbed his backpack, and then headed for the boys' locker room. Inside, Justin quickly checked his blood sugar. His blood sugar was low. Justin shook his head. He knew he was supposed to take glucose tablets to raise his blood sugar. Luckily, his mom had packed plenty of those in his backpack. Justin quickly ate them, but now he had to wait fifteen minutes. What was he supposed to do? He couldn't go outside and hang out on the sidelines. That would look weird.

So he sat on the bench and stared at his cell phone screen, watching the numbers change one by one. After five minutes, Coach Perez poked his head in the door.

"Justin, you okay?" he asked.

"My blood sugar was low," Justin replied. "I took care of it, but I've gotta check it again after fifteen minutes."

"All right," Coach Perez said. "Don't rush it, okay?"

"Okay, Coach."

The next ten minutes were the slowest

of Justin's life. All he wanted to do was get back on the court. Finally, time was up. He checked his blood sugar again and saw that it was back in the target range. Then he quickly ate a banana since he knew he had the rest of the game to play.

Justin raced back out onto the court. The scrimmage was pretty heated. Marcus was at the foul line, and Darius was guarding him closely. Logan broke free from Aaron and waved his arms in the air.

"Pass it! Pass it!"

But Darius was right in Marcus's face. Marcus faked like he was going to pass it to Logan, aimed, and then quickly spun around. In the brief second that he broke free from Darius, he shot.

Swish! Two points. The guy was good.

Marcus high-fived his teammates. Then he saw Justin.

"What's the matter, Justin? Swine flu

get you again? Oink!" he called out.

Coach Perez called out the score "That's twenty-two–six." Justin didn't have to ask which team was losing. He was pretty sure it was his.

He ran out onto the court.

"Freddy, sit out," he called. "Mike, you're back to center."

With Luis as point guard and Aaron as small forward, they had a pretty strong team. They should have been able to close the point gap. But Justin just couldn't get his head back in the game. Sitting out like that really bugged him, and he kept worrying about what the other guys thought about it. Normally, he could handle any rebound that ricocheted off the backboard. But he missed three easy ones in a row. He made a couple of shots, but he missed an easy jump shot that even Darius could have made.

Coach Perez blew his whistle at the end

of the game. "Final score, thirty-seven to nineteen."

Justin felt terrible. It was his first day as captain, and he'd lost a scrimmage. Not just lost—Marcus and his team had destroyed them. And it was all because he'd let his worries get to him. He could be the strongest physical player on the floor, but if his head wasn't in the game, that was going to cause problems.

Justin didn't talk to anybody as he headed out of the gym. He went right to his mom's car and jumped inside, slamming the door.

"How'd practice go, honey?" Mrs. Cooper asked.

Justin didn't answer her. He stared out the window the entire way to the diabetes center, and his mom didn't ask any more questions.

Chapter 6

Later that day, Justin was lying on his bed, staring at the NBA posters on his wall. He'd had a follow-up appointment with Dr. Chang at the diabetes center. She had asked a lot of questions about practice, and Justin had told her everything—except the part about how worried he got about what the other guys were thinking. Dr. Chang had a lot of helpful advice about how to keep his blood sugar from dropping during practice, but it didn't make Justin feel much better. One day his biggest worry was his math test, and the next day he was worrying about snacks and needles and glucose tablets.

"It's not fair," Justin muttered. Then he heard a knock on the door.

"Come in."

Mr. Cooper walked in holding a small envelope.

"Your mom said practice didn't go so well today. Do you want to talk about it?" he asked.

Justin sighed. "It's . . . hard to explain, okay? I'm team captain. I shouldn't have to leave in the middle of everything. I should always be there for my team."

His dad nodded. "That's got to be frustrating. I get it. But Coach Perez picked you to be captain for a lot of reasons. Not just because you play well, but because you're a good leader. And good leaders know how to adapt when things change. You've got a strong team, Justin. It's okay if you are out of the game for a few minutes."

Justin understood what his dad meant, but it didn't make him feel much better.

Mr. Cooper opened the envelope. "Your ID bracelet just came in the mail," he said.

Justin had picked out the bracelet from a catalog at one of his diabetes classes. He was supposed to wear it so that if he ever got sick, people would know he had diabetes and would be able to treat him correctly. His dad took it out of the envelope, and Justin frowned. He hadn't thought much about it when he ordered it, but now he wasn't sure if he liked the idea of wearing something that proclaimed his diabetes so loudly.

"Do I really have to wear this?" Justin asked.

"Come on, it's not so bad," Mr. Cooper said.

Justin reluctantly took the bracelet from his dad. "Can I at least take it off for practice?" he asked.

"Sorry," Mr. Cooper said. "It's especially important to wear it to practice and during games. You already know that your blood sugar can get low if you're exercising a lot. If something happens, people will need to know what's wrong so they can help you."

Justin put the bracelet on. He didn't say anything for a while.

"Okay," he said finally.

"It looks cool, really," his dad said. "I bet most people won't even notice it."

On Monday, Justin and his team started practice with a pep talk from Coach Perez.

"Wednesday is our first game of the season. We're facing the Lakewood Lightning Bolts. Last year they beat us in the championship."

Justin had been on the sixth-grade team last year, but they had all gone to see that game. The Hawks had lost in the last thirty seconds. It was pretty devastating.

"But this year's gonna be different," Coach Perez said. "We're a stronger team. I think we can take them this year. And we start now."

"Yeah!" all the players shouted, pumping their fists in the air.

Coach Perez looked pleased. "I want to go over some strategy before we start drills."

Marcus raised his hand. "Coach, why does Justin get to wear a bracelet? I thought we couldn't wear anything on the court."

I knew *someone would notice,* Justin thought, suddenly feeling angry. *Why do parents always act like everything's going to be all right, when it never is?*

Coach Perez looked at Justin, and for a horrible second he thought the coach might tell everyone about his diabetes. He eyed the bracelet.

"It's my good-luck charm," Justin said, thinking quickly. "My uncle gave it to me. He played college ball and never lost a game with it."

He was kind of surprised at how easily the lie came out.

"That's not fair," Marcus protested. "Coach, you wouldn't let me wear my lucky shark's-tooth necklace."

"That thing could put somebody's eye out," Coach Perez replied. "Drop it, Marcus. Let's focus on Wednesday's game, not our team-mates' fashion choices."

Justin wished he could thank the coach out loud. He was really helping him out. But that would only call more attention to the bracelet. Justin would have to do a better job of lying low, especially around Marcus. He was the last person Justin wanted knowing about his diabetes.

If Marcus ever found out, Justin was sure he would never hear the end of it.

Justin was walking to meet his mom after practice when Mike called him over.

"I saved up my allowance and bought that new NBA video game," he said. "Want to come over and play it? Mom says you can stay for dinner."

"Yeah!" Justin said happily. It was just what he needed to get his mind off of everything. He ran to his mom. "Mom, can I go to Mike's? His mom says it's okay."

Justin's mom got a disappointed look on her face. "Oh, honey, I'm sorry, but you have an . . . appointment," she said, glancing at Mike. She was trying to keep Justin's secret.

Justin pulled his mom aside. "Can't I just

miss this one?" he asked. "We're there, like, all the time."

"Sweetie, they're expecting us, and these first few weeks are really important," his mom said. "I'll talk to Mike's mom and make a plan for you to go over some other time."

Justin knew there was no use in arguing. He walked back to Mike. "My mom won't let me go. Sorry."

"Okay," Mike said. "Maybe we can do it this weekend."

Justin didn't answer. He stomped to the car and slammed the door behind him as he entered.

His mom turned to look at him. "I know this isn't easy. But you know what Kendra says, it's going to take some adjustment—"

"I know," Justin said crabbily. "Whatever. This stinks."

Chapter 7

"**I** can't believe tonight is your first game!" said Mrs. Cooper. "Go, Hawks, go!"

It was Wednesday, and his mom and dad were both wearing Hawks T-shirts. His mom even had black and gold pom-poms. They were driving to Lakewood for the game against the Lightning Bolts.

Justin played with his ID bracelet. Marcus had finally stopped asking about it, and Tuesday's practice had gone all right.

Justin's blood sugar had been fine every time he checked, so he hadn't needed to leave practice for too long. He was starting to get the hang of checking his blood sugar and taking his shots.

Thinking about the game had taken his mind off his diabetes. It was the first game of the season, he was team captain, and they were facing their rivals. What could be better than that?

His mom turned around in her seat to talk to him.

"I put more glucose tablets in your backpack in case your blood sugar gets low. Promise me you'll let the coach know if you're feeling low during the game."

"I promise," Justin told her.

"And make sure you—"

"Check my blood sugar during the game," Justin finished for her. "I will, Mom, I will."

The bleachers were getting crowded by

the time they reached the school gym at six thirty. On one half of the court, some of the Bolts were warming up in their white uniforms marked with yellow spears of lightning. On the other side, Mike and Freddy were passing and shooting. Justin ran to join them.

"Dude, I am so pumped for this," Mike said, bumping fists with Justin.

"Me too," Justin said. "We gotta make up for last year!"

The other Hawks joined them one by one and the team warmed up together. Just before the game started, Coach Perez gathered them all together in a huddle.

"Remember, they like to pass the ball," he said. "We can use that to our advantage. Stick with your man, make sure he can't pass. Justin, you know what to do."

"Yes, Coach!" Justin replied.

"Here's how we're starting," the coach

said. "Mike, you're my center. Marcus, point guard. Logan, shooting guard. Luis, small forward, and Justin, power forward. Got it?"

"Yes, Coach!" the players shouted.

Justin and the rest of the team ran onto the court. The ref threw the ball in the air, and the two centers leaped for it. Mike's outstretched right hand got there first. *Slam!* The ball bounced three feet in front of him, and the Bolts charged after it. Logan and Justin were the closest Hawks, and they ran for it, too. Logan reached the ball first.

Justin raced past him. One of the Bolts was right on him, and he couldn't get away. Marcus did what he did best—made a break for it.

"Logan, over here!" he called out.

Logan passed the ball to Marcus, who took a shot from just inside the three-point line. The ball hit the rim and bounced off.

Justin took a mighty leap and grabbed the ball before it could hit the court. He'd lost the man covering him and had a clear shot.

Bam! Right off the backboard into the net. Two points for the Hawks!

"Way to go, Justin!" his mom cheered from the stands.

Justin's heart was pounding. He felt great. *This* was what it was all about.

It was a good start to the game, but the Bolts were tough. They passed the ball to one another so fast, it was like a big mosquito buzzing over their heads. The Bolts' center got possession and sank a shot from the foul line.

The next half hour went like that. The Hawks were doing really well, but so were the Bolts. Justin's team usually held a four-point lead, but they knew they could lose it at any time.

The ref's whistle blew—Coach Perez was

asking for a time-out. The team huddled together for a quick change of strategy and then started to run back on the court. But Coach tapped Justin on the shoulder.

"Ryan, you're in for Justin," the coach called out, and Ryan ran onto the court.

"What's up?" Justin asked.

"It's time to check your blood sugar," Coach Perez reminded him.

Justin quickly looked behind him. Had anyone heard? Then he checked the clock.

"Already?" he asked. "But I thought I had more time."

The coach tapped his clipboard. "Your parents gave me a schedule to follow, Justin. Go ahead and check your blood sugar. I'll put you right in when you come back."

"Okay, Coach," Justin said. He hated leaving the game.

Justin had to walk all the way around the court to get to the boys' locker room. He felt like everyone was looking at him. When he got inside, he washed his hands and used the glucose monitor. His numbers were good. He was okay to play.

"What a waste of time," he muttered.

By the time he got back to the court, the tables had turned. The Bolts had a four-point lead and the first half was ending. The players came off the court.

"Yo, Justin. How was your potty break?" Marcus asked.

Justin ignored him.

"Stuff it, Marcus," Mike said quickly. "We gotta figure out how to get our lead back."

"They're good, but we're better," Coach Perez said. "We need to tighten our defense. I'm going to put Darius in."

"I won't let you down, Coach," Darius said.

The coach put Justin back in the game, too, but all the confidence he had felt before was gone. He kept thinking that everyone knew why he'd had to leave the game. They could probably read his ID bracelet from the bleachers. He saw two moms whispering to each other. They were probably talking about him. . . .

Justin was so busy worrying he didn't hear the ref's whistle or see the ball shoot right past him and out of bounds.

"Justin, wake up over there!" Marcus yelled across the court.

"Oh, sorry," Justin said. He felt like such a loser. He had to get his head back in the game.

But he couldn't. Luis got control of the ball, dribbled down the court, and took a shot. Justin was in easy reach of the rebound, but it slipped past his fingertips.

The Bolts' lead advanced by another two points. After a few more minutes, Coach Perez took Justin out and sent in Terrell in his place. Justin knew he had failed the team.

You're captain, he told himself. *Keep it together. You can still help from the sidelines.*

But he felt like a bike tire with a hole in it—he just couldn't get pumped up. He paced the sidelines for the rest of the game. The Hawks couldn't regain their lead no matter how hard they tried.

I'm just bringing down the team. If I really want to help them, I should just quit!

Chapter 8

Justin ran out of the gym as soon as the game was over. He saw his parents walking down from the bleachers, but he didn't wait for them. Instead, he headed right for the car. He just wanted to get away.

Suddenly Justin felt a tap on the shoulder. "Dude, where you going?" Mike asked. "I know we lost, but we're still going to Sal's. Maybe we can figure out where we went wrong and how we can do better next time. We came pretty close."

"No thanks," Justin said. He didn't even look at Mike. He just kept walking.

"Hey, are you okay?" Mike asked.

"I'm fine," Justin replied. "I just can't go out, that's all."

Mike watched Justin walk away. His mom was waiting outside their blue minivan. Logan, Freddy, and Darius were waiting for him, too.

"Is Justin coming?" Logan asked.

Mike shook his head. "No. Come on, let's go."

They piled into the minivan, and Mike's mom drove them to Sal's.

The delicious smell of hot pizza floated out of Sal's open door and into the parking lot. Even though it was after eight on a Wednesday night, the place was pretty crowded. The boys grabbed drinks from the refrigerator and found a table in the back of the room. Mrs. Vantine ordered a pizza for them at the counter.

"I'll be at that booth over there," she said, motioning toward the far side of the room. "Half an hour, okay? It's a school night."

"Yes, Mom," Mike said. Then he turned to his friends and made a face.

"I know what you're doing," Mrs. Vantine teased. She shook her head and walked away.

"Sorry. She never lets me stay up late," Mike apologized to his friends.

"At least she's cool enough to drive us here," Freddy said. "My mom never wants to do it."

The waiter brought over the pizza and the boys each grabbed a steaming hot slice.

"What was up with Justin today?" Logan asked. "We were winning, and then it's like he had a meltdown or something."

"Marcus says the pressure of being captain is too much for him," Freddy said, his mouth full of pizza.

"Did he also tell you that you have cheese on your jersey?" Darius asked.

The other boys cracked up as Freddy looked down at his shirt.

"It's just cheese," he said. "Anyway, I'm serious. First he's out for, like, a week. Then he comes back, but he keeps leaving in the middle of practice. Then today. I mean, what's up?"

Darius reached for a second slice of pizza.

"Dude, how fast did you eat that first one?" Mike asked. "I didn't even see you chew."

"I need to refuel," Darius said. "Anyway, Freddy's right. Something's definitely up with Justin."

"Marcus is right," Logan said. "He's cracking under pressure."

Mike shook his head. "No way. I know Justin. I think something's bothering him, but it's not being captain. He was born to be captain. He's been teaching me how to play since we were in second grade."

"Well, he better get back on track soon," Darius said. "I don't want to keep losing like we did tonight."

"Yeah, we don't want to be losers," Freddy said. "That would be—hey!"

A spitball hit him right in the cheek. Logan put down his soda straw and started laughing.

"Oh, man, bull's-eye!"

"Too bad your aim wasn't that good when you tried to make that foul shot," Darius said.

Everyone laughed but Mike. He was too busy thinking about Justin. Something was definitely wrong—he knew it. He and Justin were best friends. They told each other everything. Like that time when Kerry Peters tried to kiss him at the pool last summer — Mike had told Justin, and nobody else. So why wasn't Justin talking to him now?

A spitball hit his forehead, interrupting his thoughts.

"Dude!" Mike cried out. He threw his napkin at Logan. That's when Mike's mom showed up.

"I think it's time to end this party," she said. "Everybody finish up."

Mike was still thinking about Justin when he got home. He changed and showered, and then decided to call his friend.

Justin answered after three rings.

"What?"

"Listen," Mike said. "It's just . . . I know you said nothing's wrong. But I can tell something's bothering you. What's going on? Some of the guys on the team are talking trash."

"I don't care," Justin replied. "It's nothing, all right?"

"I don't believe you," Mike said.

"You don't have to," Justin said. "Listen, I gotta go. Mom would kill me if she knew I was on my cell phone this late. Everything's fine, okay?"

"Okay," Mike said, but he wasn't convinced.

He wished Justin would talk to him. If he kept acting weird, the other guys might really start to give him a hard time. And that would be bad for the whole team.

Chapter 9

A few days later, Justin's mom took him back to the diabetes center to meet with Kendra. Justin liked Kendra's office. Instead of posters about germs and diseases, she had pictures of animals and famous sports players on the walls. Kendra smiled when she saw Justin.

"Hey, good to see you guys," Kendra said. "Have a seat."

Justin and his mom sat down in some

soft red chairs across from Kendra.

"Dr. Chang told me about the problem you had at practice the other day," Kendra said. "One of our goals at these classes is to help you solve any problems that come up. Remember, we want to make managing your diabetes as easy as possible."

"Yeah, I remember," Justin said.

Kendra passed him a pamphlet. "I get that it's hard to be looking at the clock all the time. That's got to be distracting. But I think I have a solution for you," she said. "They sell sports watches with timers. Before you start to exercise, you can set the timer to beep when it's time to check your blood sugar. That way you'll know when to check it without having to look at the clock. I work with a lot of kids who play sports, and some of them use a watch like that. They say it helps them concentrate on the game better."

"That sounds like a good idea," Justin

agreed. Marcus would probably complain if he wore a watch, but he didn't care. It was a good solution to his problem.

"You know, a lot of the kids on the diabetes blogs talk about these watches and how helpful they are," Kendra said. "I guess you haven't checked any of them out yet, huh?"

Justin shook his head.

"What about talking to your friends or teammates?" she asked. "They can help you with stuff like this."

Justin's face clouded. "I just don't want them to know, okay?"

"That's up to you," Kendra told him. "But I bet your close friends know something is going on with you. They've probably come up with some crazy ideas about what it could be, too. The truth is a lot better."

Justin thought about Marcus and his "swine flu" jokes, and the call from Mike. But he didn't say anything.

"Just think about it, okay?" Kendra said. Justin saw his mom give Kendra a grateful look. Were they ganging up on him?

Justin shrugged. "I already thought about it."

"All right, then," Kendra said. She looked at Mrs. Cooper. "You're seeing Lisa today, right?"

Mrs. Cooper nodded. "She's going to talk to us about how to order the right food when we eat out, or if Justin is going to a party."

Justin hopped off the table. "Thanks for the watch idea," he told Kendra, eager to get on with his appointments so he could go home and look for a watch.

"You're welcome. I hope it helps."

"I know it will," Justin said. The watch would be the answer to all of his problems, he was sure. Now he would be able to focus on his game. Marcus and the other guys would stop talking trash about him—and he'd still be able to keep his secret.

Chapter 10

Justin jumped out of bed at seven a.m. on Saturday morning. The Hawks had a game against the Bricktown Hammers and he was ready! This game wasn't going to be like the last one. Not with his new watch to help him out. It had just come in the mail the day before! His mom had found a black watch with gold stitching on the wristband — Hawks colors. It was perfect.

Justin checked his blood sugar and gave

himself an insulin shot while his mom looked on. Then he ate the scrambled eggs, cantaloupe, whole wheat toast, and milk his dad made him for breakfast. Even though the game didn't start until eleven, he was in his uniform and ready to go by eight thirty.

It was a home game, and both of his parents went with him. They got to the gym at ten thirty, and Justin set the timer on his watch. He started warming up with the other players on the court immediately.

"Hey, Justin," Marcus said, passing him the ball. "You going to run to the potty again during the game today? Didn't your mommy toilet train you?"

Justin ignored him. He dribbled the ball to the basket and made the shot.

Once again, Mike stood up for him. "Stuff it, Marcus," he said as he caught the ball.

"If I were captain, I wouldn't be leaving in

the middle of a game," Marcus said loudly. "Just saying."

Justin gritted his teeth. He usually didn't let Marcus get to him—he knew he was a loudmouthed jerk.

Mike passed the ball hard to Marcus. He stumbled back a few steps as he caught it. Then he recovered and started to dribble toward the basket. Justin ran up and stole the ball from him.

"Well, you're *not* the captain," he said simply. Then he shot the ball and watched it sail through the net. Mike high-fived him.

Marcus didn't say anything. Justin felt great. He had a good feeling about this game.

Soon it was time to play. Coach had him start again, along with Mike, Marcus, Noah, and Terrell. The Hammers took the court in their red and black uniforms. They didn't have too many big guys, Justin noticed.

The whistle blew, and the game started

hard and fast. The Hammers were good ball handlers, and man, were they fast. Justin tore up and down the court, guarding his man. The Hammers tried a few shots, but Justin and Terrell managed to block each of them.

Meanwhile, the Hawks were playing a great offensive game. Mike and Marcus each scored some points, and Justin made three baskets off of rebounds within the first fifteen minutes. The game was going just as he'd planned.

And then . . . everything felt wrong. Justin's head felt light and empty, and the floor started to spin beneath his feet. He felt queasy. Was it past eleven thirty? Did the timer mess up? He looked at his watch and saw that it was only 11:17.

Then he realized—it was the same way he'd felt that first week, when he was exercising and his blood sugar was low. He remembered

Dr. Chang's advice—stop what he was doing right away, check his blood sugar, and take some glucose tablets if necessary.

The last thing in the world Justin wanted to do was leave the court. But he knew if he didn't, things would get worse. He ran to the sidelines as the ref blew the whistle.

"I'm feeling light-headed," he told Coach Perez. "I gotta take care of this."

Coach Perez nodded and then waved at Justin's parents in the stands. Justin's dad hurried down and followed him to the boys' locker room.

"You okay?" Mr. Cooper asked worriedly.

Justin sat down on the bench and checked his blood sugar. It was low. He quickly ate a few glucose tablets before answering his father.

"I think so," Justin said. "It's probably because I ate breakfast so early. I should have had a snack before the game."

Outside the locker room, they could hear the crowd cheering. The Hawks had scored again.

"So, now you wait fifteen to twenty minutes, right?" his dad asked.

Justin nodded.

"All right. I'll hang with you," Mr. Cooper said.

They sat together in silence for a few minutes, listening to the sound of feet pounding up and down the court.

"You did the right thing, leaving the game," his dad said. "I'm proud of you. I know it must have been hard to do."

"Definitely," Justin replied. "I want to be out there playing, not sitting in here."

"It's going to get easier," his dad said. "Kendra says it takes practice in the beginning to figure this stuff out. Next time, we'll remember that you need a snack before the game."

"Maybe," Justin said, but he wasn't convinced. Everything seemed so complicated.

Justin checked his blood sugar again when it was time.

"I'm good," he told his dad, showing him the meter. "But I'm going to eat a granola bar and have some juice to keep my blood sugar up so I can go back out there."

"All right," Mr. Cooper said when Justin had finished his snack. "Get back out there and lead your team to victory!"

Justin ran back into the gym. It was almost halftime. Coach Perez kept him out of the game until the half was over.

The players came off of the court. "Yo, it's Captain Quitter!" Marcus called out, and some of the guys laughed.

"I'm not quitting," Justin said.

Coach Perez looked at him. "You good to go out in the next half?"

Justin nodded in reply.

The coach clapped his hands together. "Okay. Keep doing what you're doing. Don't let up!"

Justin ran onto the court for the second half. He glanced at the scoreboard and saw that the Hawks were winning, 35–12. It was a great lead.

But the confidence he'd had at the beginning of the game was gone. The second half picked up at the same crazy pace as before, but this time Justin was distracted. He messed up and let three guys score in a row. After five minutes Coach Perez took him out and put in Freddy in his place. Justin watched the end of the half from the sidelines.

"Sorry, Justin," Coach Perez told him. "I know you're not feeling well."

But Justin was feeling fine now. The diabetes wasn't his problem, and he knew it. His confidence had taken a vacation. That's why his game was hurting.

In the end, the Hawks still won. The players came off the court, cheering and high-fiving each other.

"Great game, guys!" Coach Perez said.

"No thanks to Justin," Marcus muttered.

Justin didn't say anything. He couldn't.

Marcus was right.

Chapter II

That Monday at school, Justin was really quiet. He and Mike both had first period English with Ms. McMahon. During class, Jeremy Kim sneezed and got snot all over his math book. Everyone was cracking up, even Jeremy, but when Mike looked at Justin, he wasn't even laughing. Something was definitely bugging him.

As they left class, Mike thought about asking him again what was wrong. But what was the point? Justin probably wouldn't tell him.

Mike had a science test that morning, and he forgot about Justin for a while. Just before lunch, he was walking past the front office when Mrs. Hillstrand, the school secretary, called his name.

"Can you please take this to Nurse Myers?" she asked, handing him an envelope.

"Sure," Mike said. He stuck the envelope under his arm and made a left turn down the hall. He jogged all the way to the nurse's office. He didn't want to be late for lunch — today was chicken nugget day.

The nurse's office door was closed, so Mike pushed it open. Then he froze. Justin and Nurse Myers were over by a table, and Justin was sticking some kind of needle in his leg.

"Oh, um, hey, Justin," Mike said awkwardly.

Justin looked up, startled. "Dude, a little privacy!"

Mike wasn't sure what to do. "I didn't mean — I just have to drop off this envelope."

Justin didn't say anything.

"All right then. See you at lunch," Mike said, and he quickly ran out of the office.

Justin headed for his locker to get the lunch his mom had packed. He was worried.

Mike hadn't asked him about the shot, but Justin knew he must be wondering about it. Justin took his lunch bag out of his locker and shut the door. He thought about what Kendra had told him.

I bet your close friends know something is going on with you. They've probably come up with some crazy ideas about what it could be, too. The truth is a lot better.

Justin knew deep down that Kendra was right. But how was he supposed to tell

Mike? What was he supposed to say?

Justin thought about what happened all afternoon. Mike was sure to ask him about the shot. He didn't want to lie again. He didn't feel like keeping the secret from the team anymore, either.

He was the captain, after all. Captains didn't keep secrets. They had to earn the trust of their teammates. And now, everyone was suspicious of him.

And all that worrying was affecting his game, too. He thought back to the game against the Hammers. Yeah, he hated having to leave the game. But his diabetes didn't cause him to play badly when he came back. His own brain did that to him.

By the time practice came, Justin made up his mind. He thought he might tell everyone before practice started, but he couldn't get the words out. He led a great practice, focusing on the drills.

"Good practice tonight, guys," Coach Perez told everyone when practice was done. "I'm feeling really good about your next game."

"Coach, I'd like to say something," Justin said.

"Sure, Justin," Coach Perez said with a nod.

Justin wasn't sure where to start. He looked at Mike.

"So, I know you guys think I've been acting weird lately," he said. "And I want to tell you what's up. A few weeks ago I found out I have type 1 diabetes. I guess I've had a lot on my mind lately, and it's throwing me off my game. I'm trying to stop that, but I thought you should know what's going on. So that's the deal."

He waited for a response, but nobody said anything. Everyone looked kind of confused.

"Justin's been doing a great job managing

his diabetes and being captain of this team at the same time," Coach Perez said.

"That's cool," Mike said finally.

None of the other guys said anything. Justin suddenly felt awkward.

"Okay, see you tomorrow, then," he said quickly. Then he jogged out to find his mom's car in the parking lot.

Had he done the right thing?

Chapter 12

Justin has diabetes. The thought kept running through Mike's head. He thought that might be what it was when he saw Justin giving himself the shot. His cousin Connor had diabetes, too. He had been diagnosed with it four years ago, when he was twelve. Mike was just a little kid then, but he remembered seeing Connor prick his finger with something. It looked kind of scary.

"What are you doing?" Mike had asked.

Connor had explained everything. He had diabetes and that meant he had to check his blood a lot and take shots every day. But he wasn't sick, and he wasn't going to die or anything. After a while, Mike even forgot Connor had it. He was the same old Connor. He played basketball, too, and was on his high school team.

When practice ended, Mike ran out to the parking lot and jumped in the passenger seat of his mom's minivan.

"Mom, can we go to Aunt Suzy's?" he asked.

His mom looked puzzled. "Why do you want to go there?"

"I need to talk to Connor," Mike said. "Remember how I was telling you Justin's been acting weird?"

Mrs. Vantine nodded.

"Well, today I saw him in the nurse's office shooting a needle into his leg," Mike told her. "And at practice just now, he told us he has diabetes, like Connor. I just thought . . . maybe Connor can help somehow."

"You'd better text him and make sure he's home," she said. "He might have practice."

Mike pulled out his cell phone and quickly texted his cousin. *Dude, need 2 talk 2 u. U home?*

The reply came quickly. *In my room, studying for bio. C u soon, cuz.*

"He's there," Mike said.

His mom started the car. "Then let's go. I think talking to Connor is a great idea."

Mike's cousin lived in Bricktown, so it didn't take long to get there. His aunt Suzy was working, but his mom stayed downstairs and made herself a cup of tea. Mike needed to talk to Connor alone.

His cousin was sitting on his bed with a

laptop on his lap, wearing his red and black Hammers uniform. He looked up from the screen when Mike came into the room.

"So, what's so important?" Connor asked.

"You know my friend Justin?" Mike asked him.

Connor nodded. "Sure. That kid is really good at basketball."

"He has diabetes, like you," Mike said. "He's been acting weird for a while, and he hasn't been playing well—like something's on his mind. He just told me and the team today. But he's still acting really worried about it."

"Sounds like me when I first got diagnosed," Connor said.

"Really?" Mike asked. He sat down on the edge of the bed.

"It really stinks in the beginning," Connor said. "I was scared I could never play basketball again. I was worried the guys would think I would bring down the team. Maybe Justin feels the same way."

"Some of the guys were talking trash about him before he told us what was wrong," Mike said. "I think they'll stop now. But everyone seemed kind of confused when Justin told us."

Connor nodded. "It can be really confusing. But the more they know, the less confusing it will be."

Mike was thoughtful for a minute. Then he had an idea.

"Can you be at Sal's tomorrow around five?" he asked his cousin.

"Sure," Connor said. "My game doesn't start until eight. Why, what's up?"

Mike told Connor his plan, and Connor agreed to show up at the pizza place.

The next afternoon, Mike got all the guys on the team—except for Justin—to go to

Sal's after practice. Connor was waiting for them when they got there.

The boys sat at the longest table in the place, at the back of the room. The waiter came by and they ordered two large pizzas and drinks.

"This is my cousin Connor," Mike explained. "He plays for the Hammers high school team."

"No way!" Marcus said. "You guys are awesome. My older brother's team played you guys last week. You totally creamed them."

"They played a good game," Connor said. "But yeah, we're a good team. Thanks."

"So, Connor's here because I wanted to talk to you guys about something," Mike said. "About Justin and his diabetes. Connor has diabetes, too."

"Isn't diabetes when your blood is messed up?" Freddy asked.

"Not exactly," Connor replied. "There's an organ in your body called your pancreas. It makes something called insulin that controls your blood sugar. For kids with type 1, like me, the pancreas doesn't make insulin. So I have to inject it into my body every day."

Marcus looked thoughtful. "Is that why he keeps leaving games?"

"Probably," Connor said. "If I'm exercising a lot, I have to stop to check my blood sugar."

"But you're a great player," Marcus said. "Every time Justin comes back in the game, it's like he's forgotten how to play."

"Diabetes can be confusing in the beginning," Connor said. "I remember that sometimes I got distracted when I was playing. But I learned to deal with it. You guys need to give Justin some time."

Everybody was quiet for a moment.

"He's probably worried about what you're thinking, too," Connor said. "I thought nobody would want to be around me. But once they saw I was the same Connor, nobody cared anymore. If I had quit when I got diabetes, I wouldn't be where I am today. I'm a power forward on the team. I use that to motivate myself. I power forward in life with my diabetes. I didn't let it stop me. And it won't stop Justin."

"See?" Mike said. "We need to help Justin get his game back. We have to show him we're okay with his diabetes."

Mike looked right at Marcus. "We've got to stick together if we want to be a strong team."

Marcus looked a little embarrassed. "He should have told us sooner," he muttered.

Freddy wiped some tomato sauce from his face. "So what are we supposed to do?"

"We should talk to him at practice

tomorrow," Mike said. "Tell him that his diabetes is cool with us."

Marcus was thoughtful. "What do you guys think about this?" he began.

Chapter 13

The next afternoon, Justin headed down the hall to the gym, eating a banana to help him get through practice. He was a little nervous. He had been avoiding his teammates since his big announcement yesterday. He even thought he saw Marcus and Mike whispering and looking his way at lunch. Were they talking about him?

It didn't matter. His secret was out. He had diabetes, and the guys were just going to have to deal with it. He walked through the doors confidently—and got the second biggest surprise of his life.

His teammates were lined up right behind the door. Each one of them was wearing a yellow T-shirt with big black letters that read, POWER FORWARD WITH DIABETES. Justin stopped, stunned. He had no idea what to say.

Marcus stepped forward. "The T-shirts were my idea," he bragged. "My dad owns the T-shirt shop at the mall."

"Yeah, we just want to let you know that we don't care if you have diabetes," Mike said. "We'll help out in any way we can!"

Justin paused for a second. "They're cool," he said. "And you guys really don't care?"

"No way," Mike said. He handed Justin a T-shirt. "Here's yours."

Justin held his up.

"Turn it around," Marcus told him.

Justin did. His shirt said CAPTAIN on the back.

For a second Justin thought he might cry, but that would be even worse than having diabetes. So he started talking. The words poured out of him.

"Yeah, so, I can still play and everything," he said. "The wristband is an ID bracelet in case I get sick. And the watch has a timer in it. When it goes off, I have to check my blood sugar. Sometimes I can get back into the game right away, and sometimes I can't."

"Whatever," Freddy said. "Coach can put me in instead."

Everybody laughed. "That's cool," Justin said. "I know you guys can handle things without me for a few minutes."

Marcus rolled his eyes. "What is this, the Oprah show or something? When are we gonna practice?"

"Right now," Coach Perez said. "Justin,

let's start with some defensive drills. We're facing Lakewood again next week, and we need to make sure they don't score."

"Yes, Coach!" Justin said. "Just need to change my shirt."

Justin took off his practice T-shirt and put on his Power Forward shirt. Then he ran out onto the court. He stopped when he passed Mike.

"Hey, man, thanks," he said.

Mike grinned. "No problem, dude."

"Thirty seconds on the clock!" Coach Perez called out.

It was the Hawks versus the Lightning Bolts, and the score was 33–33. The Bolts had the ball, and the player Justin was covering was in scoring range. He stopped, looking for a chance to pass or shoot. But Justin was on him like glue.

The guy spun around like a top and went

113

for a jump shot. Justin leaped into the air, stretching his arms as high as he could. The ball was his! As soon as his feet landed he charged down the court.

"Go, Justin, go!" his mom and dad cheered from the stands.

Two Bolts players were gaining on him from either side. Justin knew he'd have to act fast. He came to a stop right at the free throw line and sent the ball sailing through the air.

Swish! Nothing but net! The next sound Justin heard was the ref's whistle blowing.

"Game over! The Hawks win by two points!"

Marcus ran up to him and slapped his hand. "Nice one, Justin."

"Thanks," Justin replied.

He was on top of the world. His confidence was back. And with the help of his teammates, he felt like he could handle almost anything—even his diabetes.

Questions to Think About

1. When Justin is first diagnosed, he has a lot of questions. What were you most curious about? How did you go about finding answers to your questions?

2. Justin thinks about telling his friends about his diabetes right away, but decides against it. Why do you think

that is? Did you tell your friends right away or did you wait? How did they react when you told them?

3. Justin is concerned that his diabetes will prevent him from playing basketball. Did you have worries when you were first diagnosed? What were they? Who did you talk to about them? Do you still have worries?

4. Justin's social worker suggests that he talk to other kids with diabetes online, or meet with a support group. Why do you think he isn't interested in doing either? Do you know other kids who have diabetes? Does talking to them help?

5. When Justin finds out he can't play basketball for a week, he feels like

diabetes is ruining his life. Have you ever felt that way? How did you deal with the feeling?

6. Justin is surprised to find that he enjoys working out a meal plan with his mom. Do you help out with planning your meals? What changed about your eating? How do you work in your favorite foods?

7. When does Justin experience his first low? How does he handle it? Do you remember your first low? How did you feel about it?

8. Justin worries that his teachers will treat him differently when he goes back to school. What were you worried about when you returned to school? How did your first day back go?

117

9. At his first practice back, Justin can't take his eyes off the clock. What sort of obstacles did you encounter when you were first diagnosed? How have you learned to overcome them?

10. Justin attends a lot of diabetes education classes, and is even surprised to realize that he enjoys some of them. Did you attend class when you were first diagnosed? When you have questions now, whom do you talk to?

11. Kendra and Justin work together to build a schedule for when he should check his blood sugar. Did you help to build a schedule for yourself? How has it changed as you've learned to manage your diabetes?

12. Justin is upset that he has to think about everything he eats. What sort of adjustments did you have to make when you were first diagnosed? How did you deal with that?

13. Justin has to skip hanging out with Mike to go to a diabetes class. Did you ever have to miss something you wanted for diabetes appointments? How did that make you feel? How did you deal with those feelings?

14. Kendra tells Justin that they can make diabetes work with his life, not make his life work with diabetes. Did you find that to be true for you? What challenges did you face in adjusting to diabetes? Who helped you to resolve them?